The Dachshund

by William R. Sanford and Carl R. Green

Edited by Julie Bach

CRESTWOOD HOUSE

New York

Collier Macmillan Canada

Toronto

Maxwell Macmillan International Publishing Group

New York   Oxford   Singapore   Sydney

LIBRARY OF CONGRESS CATALOGING-IN-PUBLICATION DATA

Sanford, William R. (William Reynolds), 1927-
The dachshund / by William R. Sanford and Carl R. Green; edited
by Julie Bach.—1st ed.
    p.   cm.—(Top dog series)
    Includes index.
    Summary: Discusses the history, physical characteristics, care, and breeding of this
long-bodied dog, originally used for the hunting of small mammals.
    ISBN 0-89686-530-4
    1. Dachshund—Juvenile literature. [1. Dachshund.   2. Dogs.]
I. Green, Carl R.   II. Bach, Julie S., 1963-   III. Title.
IV. Series: Top dog (Crestwood House)
SF429.D25S33   1990
636.7'53—dc20   90-34058
                                                                                          CIP
                                                        636.7   AC
                                                        SAN

PHOTO CREDITS *1068*

Cover: Peter Arnold, Inc.: (Gerard Lacz)
Animals Animals: (Margot Conte) 4, 21; (Robert Pearcy)
    11; (Margot Bruhmuller) 16; (Richard Kolar) 25
Kevin J. Nolan: 6, 28, 31
Berg & Associates: (Margaret C. Berg) 8, 12
Chandoha Photography: (Walter Chandoha) 15, 27, 32, 37
Reynolds Photography: (Larry Reynolds) 19, 22
DRK Photo: (Don and Pat Valenti) 35
Michael Reed: 39, 41, 44

Macmillan Publishing Company   Collier Macmillan Canada, Inc.
866 Third Avenue   1200 Eglinton Avenue East
New York, NY 10022   Suite 200
                                                                 Don Mills, Ontario M3C 3N1

CRESTWOOD HOUSE

Printed in the United States of America

First Edition

10   9   8   7   6   5   4   3   2   1

◤CONTENTS

For more information about dachshunds, write to:

Dachshund Club of America
c/o Julia Goulder
7540 Silvercrest Way
Scottsdale, AZ 85253
(602) 948-1144

DAXL AND BERGL

On a fall morning in the late 1800s, a woodcutter pounded on Herr Corneli's door. Corneli was the manager of a hunting preserve owned by a German nobleman.

"You must come," the woodcutter said. "A little dog is lying next to a stone on the forest floor. He looks like one of your missing dogs. I tried to bring him to you, but he wouldn't come. He growled at me when I picked him up."

Corneli's two dachshunds, Daxl and Bergl, had disappeared during a hunt five days before. As usual, the dogs had ranged ahead and out of sight. At first Corneli hadn't been alarmed. Daxl and Bergl often ran ahead to find game. But always before, they'd barked to let him know where they were. This time he'd waited till nightfall. No dogs had barked. The hunter had spent the past five days searching for the dogs. He'd also left word with all the local woodcutters and foresters that his dogs were missing.

Now Corneli grabbed his coat and hurried after the woodcutter. Maybe Daxl and Bergl were still alive!

Dachshunds are brave, energetic dogs that make excellent pets and good hunters.

Fearless swimmers, dachshunds enjoy playing in the water.
This one happily fetches a stick.

When they reached the stone, Corneli found Bergl lying next to it. The dachshund was exhausted and half starved. The little dog managed to wag his tail and lick his master's hands. But then he returned to the stone and began to dig frantically.

The two men pushed the stone aside. Under it they found the entrance to a fox den. As they listened they heard a feeble whine. It was Daxl!

Five days earlier, Daxl had chased the fox down the hole. When he dug after the fox, the stone shifted. It rolled over the opening, trapping Daxl and the fox inside.

Now Daxl crawled out. He and Bergl greeted each other joyfully. Inside the den Corneli found the fox's bones. Daxl had survived by killing the fox and eating it. But the fox had fought hard. Bite marks covered Daxl's head and flanks. Poor Bergl had suffered almost as much. He had starved for five days, waiting faithfully for his friend.

As Corneli wrote later, the experience was a "beautiful tribute to these animals." He'd always known that dachshunds were brave hunters. Now he knew they were also capable of great loyalty and devotion.

FROM HUNTER TO HOUSE PET

The word "dachshund" comes from two German words: *dachs*, which means badger, and *hund*, which means dog. It is pronounced DOCKS-hoond. Like all domesticated dogs, it belongs to the species *Canis familiaris*. It eats meat, as all dogs do.

For more than two hundred years, hunters like Herr Corneli have used dachshunds to trap *badgers*, wild *boar*, and foxes. The dogs'

7

long bodies and short legs made them especially good at hunting animals that burrow underground. A dachshund could follow a badger into a tunnel, then hold it there and bark until the hunters found it.

Dachshunds have been called "earth dogs" because their bellies hang so close to the ground. Their low-slung bodies and keen sense of smell make them excellent trackers. Even though they are the smallest and weakest of the hunting dogs, many hunters think dachshunds are the most courageous.

Strong legs and a muscular chest help the dachshund run fast and burrow into the ground after rabbits and badgers.

There are three kinds of dachshunds. Short-haired dachshunds were the first kind commonly known. Their short front legs made them good at tunneling, but their short hair couldn't protect them from bites and thorns. Long-haired dachshunds didn't have that problem. Their silky coats protected them from brambles, rain, and cold. But their coats could become heavily matted with mud in the tunnels, slowing them down. The last type of dachshunds were the wire-haired. Their bristly coats repelled rain, mud, and thorns. They were the least glamorous looking, but they were the best hunters.

The first dachshund club was formed in 1881 in England. The English took the dachshund to their hearts and turned the *breed* from hunters to pets. Most people weren't interested in hunting. They wanted a good house pet. Dachshunds didn't shed, and they were intelligent and appealing. Even Queen Victoria had dachshunds for pets.

Americans loved the dachshund, too. The breed became very popular in the United States. Then, during World War I, Americans grew suspicious of anything German. They changed the name of sauerkraut to "liberty cabbage." They called dachshunds "badger dogs." After the war, however, the breed came back into favor. Members of the armed forces brought puppies home from Germany as pets.

In 1972 the dachshund served as the mascot for the Olympic Games when they were held in Munich, Germany. Dachshunds now rank among the ten most popular breeds in the United States. They are prized as courageous and independent pets.

THE DACHSHUND IN CLOSE-UP

Dachshunds look small because they are built so close to the ground. Their legs are short compared to most dogs. A typical dachshund measures only five to nine inches from the *withers* to the ground. But try lifting this little dog, and you'll be surprised. A standard dachshund can weigh up to 28 pounds. That's as much as a two-year-old child. A miniature weighs up to 10 pounds.

Dachshunds are compact and muscular. Their chests are big because they were

Dachshunds are popular house pets because they do not shed.

originally bred to hunt. Large chests allowed room for big lungs and big hearts. When they cornered a badger underground, dachshunds needed strength to hold out against their prey. They also needed enough endurance to keep on barking until diggers located them.

Just like their ancestors, dachshunds have three different kinds of coats. Sleek and long, the smooth-haired dachshund has earned the nickname "sausage dog." It does look just like a rolled sausage. Long-haired dachshunds have soft coats with straight or slightly wavy hair.

The dachshund's long body makes some people think of hot dogs or sausages!

Seen at a distance, the third kind, the wire-haired dachshund, seems to have a smooth coat. But pet one and you'll feel the difference. The wiry hair is bristly. The wire-haired dachshund also has bushy eyebrows and a beard.

Dachshunds come in many colors. The most common are red and shades of red, tan, chocolate, gray, and black. Dachshunds can also be *brindled* (a kind of striping) and *dappled* (a light color with darker, irregular patches). A common two-color dachshund is called the black-and-tan. These dogs are black with tan markings. Some have a white spot on their chests.

When dachshunds walk, they often look as though they're waddling. But a well-bred and healthy dachshund is actually agile and vigorous. Its back is almost level, and its chest is close to the ground. Its tail is fairly short, straight, and strong. Its head is long and tapers to a narrow *muzzle.*

The dachshund's ears are broad and rounded. They are set far back on the head to keep them safe from the jaws of the dog's prey. The 42 adult teeth are the teeth of a hunter. They are sharp, strong, and fit close together in the powerful jaw.

The dachshund's dark, oval eyes don't look as if they were meant to hunt prey. They are soft and expressive. When a dachshund looks at you, your heart is apt to melt.

THE DACHSHUND'S SENSES

Imagine your nose being a million times more sensitive to smells than it is now. If someone gave you a sweater to smell, you would be able to sniff out its owner. A dog has that ability. It has 40 times more brain cells for recognizing scents than you do.

Dachshunds are known for their good noses. They can sniff out prey in thick bushes and sort out its tracks when the animal goes underground. Dachshunds are closely related to bloodhounds, another breed known for good noses. Bloodhounds have been used by police to sniff out clues and to track criminals. Although most dachshunds now are kept as household pets rather than used as hunters, they still sniff everything they can.

Dachshunds also have excellent ears. They can detect sounds up to four times farther

Dachshunds have excellent hearing and can pick up many sounds that people can't.

away than most humans can. They can hear a wider range of sounds, too. That's why they are able to hear silent dog whistles that are too highly pitched for humans to hear.

Dachshunds make good watchdogs. They may not be very big, but let the stranger beware who invades their territory. Dachshunds can make enough racket to wake the soundest sleeper. Their loud, persistent bark is another example of their origin as hunting dogs. Dachshund *breeders* refer to this barking ability as a "loud tongue."

A dachshund's eyes give it a different picture of the world than what humans see. Dogs can't see colors like we do. They can, however, see well in dim light. They don't see things far away well, either, but they are sensitive to movements in the distance. This is typical of many hunting breeds. The placement of a dachshund's eyes also influences its vision. The eyes are set on the side of the head and on a slant. This position leaves only a small field of view directly ahead where the two eyes focus on a simple object.

A dog's eye has something a human's doesn't—a third eyelid called a *haw*. You can see a small part of it in the corner of a dachshund's eye near its nose. This extra eyelid acts like a windshield wiper to clear out dust or grit.

People disagree about whether dogs are smart. With its smaller brain, a dog doesn't reason the way humans do. But dogs can learn. A dog will learn to roll over if it is rewarded with a treat each time it performs the trick. Dog trainers measure a dog's intelligence by how quickly it learns. By this standard, dachshunds do very well. When they want to, they can learn easily. But just like humans, sometimes a dachshund will choose not to obey. This has nothing to do with intelligence.

These dachshunds have found a shady place to keep out of the sun.

This has to do with another of the dachshund's traits—stubbornness!

A DACHSHUND'S MANY VOICES

Barking is the main way dogs talk. A deep, hollow bark, for instance, may be a warning. Perhaps your dachshund is telling you that a stranger is near. A high-pitched, rapid bark may indicate fear. The sound is like a fire alarm. It's hard to ignore.

Barking can be an expression of joy, as well. Your pet gets excited and barks when lots of people are around or when it's playing. Sometimes it just wants attention. If it needs you, it barks to say "I'm here!" A dachshund talks to other dogs this way, too. Dogs recognize each other's barks, even when they can't see each other.

A dog's growl isn't hard to interpret. It is a sound deep in the throat that warns possible enemies of the dog's power. The growl doesn't mean the dog is going to attack, however.

A dachshund that is left alone will be unhappy and may whine or cry.

When a dog does go after an enemy, the growl becomes more like a roar.

An unhappy dog will whine just as an unhappy child will. Usually a whine means that your pet can't do something it wants to do. A dog shut up in a room away from the family, or a puppy recently separated from its mother, is likely to whine.

A yelp is a short, high sound a dog makes in reaction to pain or loud noise. Another dog sound is the squeal. This is a high, excited, vibrating sound that shows delight and surprise.

A dog's howl is a reminder that dogs descended from wolves. Wolves use howling as a kind of gathering signal in hunting. Dogs still have that sense of being part of a pack. That's why one dog's howling can cause others in the neighborhood to join in. In fact, if you howl, you can start a dog howling. A dog that isn't used to music may howl if it hears you play the piano or begin to sing. A lonely or deserted dog will also howl. It's as if it's saying to other dogs, "I need company. Let's hear from you out there."

Dogs have their special ways of communicating. When you get to know your dog well, you can understand its different voices. This kind of listening is similar to the way a new mother learns to interpret her baby's cries.

A DOG WITH PERSONALITY

A dachshund's courage is one of its most basic traits. Even though most dachshunds no longer hunt, their old *instincts* are still there.

Dachshunds will attack any dog, no matter how large.

Digging is part of the breed's hunting instinct, too. A dachshund loves to dig holes wherever it can. Keep an eye on the flower beds! You might also notice a sleeping dachshund making scratching or digging motions on the carpet. It's still after that badger!

Dachshunds are curious about everything. They like to carry off objects that interest them. The sight of a short-legged dachshund

Dachshunds are intelligent dogs that are curious about everything going on around them.

Dachshunds come in several colors and varieties. This is a wire-haired dachshund.

making off with a fuzzy pink slipper is bound to make you smile. Some breeders describe dachshunds as natural clowns who make fine, fun-loving pets. Once in a while, this playfulness can be a drawback, however. Three puppies left alone in an apartment for a few hours can do more damage than a hurricane.

A dachshund's independence can be a challenge, as well. It can find ways to get around doing most anything it doesn't want to do. To train one successfully, you have to win it over, not just show it who's boss. Once the dachshund becomes devoted to you, it will be cooperative, faithful, and loving.

The dachshund is a dog of contrasts. It's a small dog that will attack an enemy of any size. It's strong and active but loves to sleep and easily grows fat. No one knows how these traits developed. Perhaps the nobles who required dachshunds to perform dangerous hunting tasks spoiled the little dogs between hunts.

Whatever their faults, dachshunds make wonderful pets. They keep you on your toes and leave you wondering what's coming next.

CHOOSING A DACHSHUND

Having a dog can be lots of fun. But it is also a major investment of time and money. A *purebred* dachshund, for example, costs $300 or more. Then there are licensing fees, veterinary bills, and food costs. You will have to spend time *grooming* your dog and exercising it every day.

If you do decide you're ready for a dog, you're ready for a dachshund. Dachshunds are small, clean, and easy to groom. They need fresh air, as most dogs do, but they can handle all climates.

Dachshunds do pose one special problem, however. If you live in a house or apartment with lots of stairs, a dachshund may not be the best dog for you. With its short legs and long back, it will have trouble climbing stairs. In fact, some dachshunds have developed serious spinal injuries from hauling themselves up flights of stairs.

Once you've decided a dachshund is right for you, ask yourself these questions:

Should I buy from a breeder or a pet store? Puppies at a pet store may have traveled long distances and may not be in their best condition. Also, a pet store usually has only one or two puppies to choose from. A breeder often has several different *litters* from which to choose. A buyer can also watch how the puppy behaves with its littermates. Both pet stores and breeders provide an American Kennel Club registration, with the dog's *pedigree*. These papers list the dachshund's ancestors back to great-grandparents or even further. They also have the dog's medical records and detailed care and feeding instructions.

Is it better to buy a male or a female? If you want to raise puppies, you'll want a female.

24

Females are a little more expensive than males, and they go into *heat* twice a year. This is the time they're ready to mate. All the male dogs in the neighborhood will be attracted to them. On the other hand, male dogs tend to roam more than females. But both males and females are loyal, playful, and intelligent and make good pets.

How do I choose the right dachshund? Watch all the puppies in a litter and see how they react to each other and to you. Eventually their individual personalities will shine through. Look for the one that suits you. Is it

Choosing what kind of dachshund you want as a pet is a big decision. Just remember, the dog you take home will require a lot of care.

the quiet one that seeks you out to be petted? Or is it the go-getter that jumps out of the box to see what's going on? One special dog usually catches your eye. When that happens, your choice is easy.

TRAINING YOUR DACHSHUND

You've chosen your new dachshund puppy and brought him home. You've decided Fritz would be a good name. Now you want to train him. Remember, the dachshund is very independent. To train one, your first step is to make it so attached and devoted to you that it would *rather* do things your way. That's a better approach than simply expecting the dog to obey your commands.

An untrained dog is a nuisance to others and a danger to itself. It's important to start teaching a dog as soon as it is brought home. At first, avoid places where you have to say "No" all the time. If you don't want the dog to jump on the furniture, don't let it in the living room. When you have to leave the dog alone in

Once you bring a puppy home, you will need to begin training it to obey commands like "Sit" and "Stay."

Most young dachshunds enjoy chewing on sticks, bones, and other toys.

the house, put it in a small room with its toys and nothing else to chew on. Some owners keep their dogs in playpens during the first few weeks.

Of course, sometimes you *will* have to say "No." No one can keep a puppy away from temptation forever. Be sure you scold it right after it has done something wrong. If you wait too long, the dog won't understand why it is being punished.

Commands must be simple and consistent. If you want to teach the dachshund to stay, always use the same command. Words are just sounds to a dog, so your tone of voice is important. If it hears you say "Bad dog" in a soft, gentle voice, the dog won't know it has misbehaved.

Housebreaking a puppy takes patience. The key is to anticipate the dog's needs. Dogs most often relieve themselves when they awaken and after they eat. Watch for signs like circling and sniffing the floor, and then carry the dog outside immediately. Wait until the dog is finished and then praise it. If there are accidents—and there usually are—the puppy should not be spanked or have its nose rubbed in the mess. If you catch it right afterward, scold it and take it outdoors.

Another lesson your dachshund should learn is to give something to you when you ask for it—the favorite shoe it's been chewing on, for example. If you try to pull the item away, chances are the dog will growl and defend its treasure. Remember that all dogs are pack animals. Their instincts are to defend their food and territory. As the pack leader for your dog, tell it to drop or let go, in a loud, firm voice.

A good owner wants to train a dog but not break its spirit. Rewards are as important as punishment. If you treat your puppy with firmness and love, it will learn to obey without losing its good-natured independence.

CARING FOR A DACHSHUND

A dachshund needs love and care. That means feeding, grooming, and exercising it. It also means making sure the dog has regular medical care, including shots. A good *veterinarian* will be a friend to both you and your dog.

Puppies eat more often than adult dogs do. A twelve-week-old puppy eats five times a day. As it gets older, it will eat fewer meals. A one-year-old eats only once a day. Most canned and dry dog foods have the balanced diet a dachshund needs. Dachshunds of any age always need water available in a clean dish.

Never give your dog small bones, especially chicken bones. Only large "knuckle" bones are safe because they won't splinter. Also, it's not a good idea to feed your dog from the table. Dachshunds will eat practically anything you give them! They'll get fat if you're not careful.

A short-haired dachshund is easy to groom, especially with a *hound glove*. This is a glove that has short bristles, wires, or rubber bumps set into it. Long-haireds and wire-haireds need more grooming. Use a comb on them. Also, you

A dachshund's favorite place is usually outdoors.

or a professional groomer should clip their coats every six to eight weeks.

When you bathe your dog, use a special dog shampoo. Long-haired dachshunds should be washed after grooming, or the tangles in the coat get worse. Also, a dachshund's nails should be checked from time to time. Use a hand file to keep them short and well groomed. Be careful not to injure the quick, the flesh under the nail.

Every dog needs regular exercise, but dachshunds need less than large breeds. Your dachshund will exercise itself in the backyard, but it needs to be walked, too. This also helps keep it from getting fat. A healthy dog is alert and bright-eyed, with a shiny coat. If any changes you see in your dachshund worry you, take it to the veterinarian to see if there is a problem.

Because of their short legs and long backs, dachshunds easily develop spinal problems. They can even become partially paralyzed. Don't train your dachshund to jump too high, and don't lift the dog by its front legs. Also,

Because dachshunds have such long bodies and short legs, they easily develop back problems.

keep it away from long flights of stairs. If your dog does develop a spinal problem, take it to a veterinarian. A partially paralyzed dachshund can sometimes be fitted with a cart that looks like a small luggage carrier. Its hind end rides while its front end walks.

BREEDING YOUR FEMALE DACHSHUND

If you own a female dachshund, you may decide you'd like her to have puppies. Pure-bred dachshund puppies are cute, fun, and can be valuable. But they can take a lot of work and be expensive, too.

Your female's first heat will probably occur when she is six to eight months old. It's best not to breed her during the first heat. She'll have a better chance of delivering good-sized, healthy pups if she waits. Female dogs, called *bitches*, usually go into heat twice a year.

Of course, you don't have to breed your female dachshund. Your veterinarian can *spay* her. This simple operation prevents your dog from ever getting pregnant. It costs about $100. You can also make sure your male dog doesn't make a female dog pregnant. Your vet can *neuter* him. That operation costs about the same as spaying does.

Picking the right mate, or *stud*, for your dog is important. He will have as much to do with the quality of the puppies as the female will. He should be registered with the American Kennel Club. Otherwise, the puppies will be less valuable.

One of the best ways to pick a stud is to talk to the breeder who sold you your dog. A veterinarian can help, too. These people will probably know of a good match for your dachshund. Stud owners will want to make sure the female is healthy and has had all of her shots. They will also ask for a stud fee equal to the price of a good puppy. Sometimes the stud owner will ask for "pick of the litter" instead of a fee.

The best time to mate a female is 10 to 12 days after she first shows signs of being in heat. Stud owners usually want the female taken to their kennels. Females on their home territory tend to be too aggressive.

If all goes well, you may begin to see signs in about four weeks that your dog is pregnant. A few dogs, however, show no signs until the

Your dachshund will need to have extra protein in her daily diet while she is pregnant.

puppies are born. That's why it's a good idea to have her checked by your veterinarian. Feed a pregnant dog extra protein such as cheese, milk, and eggs in addition to her regular dog food. Exercise her gently.

After your dog has mated, she must be confined at least 21 days. If she isn't, she might mate with another male of any breed. That can result in some strange-looking crossbreed puppies!

BIRTH OF A DACHSHUND PUPPY

On the average, a dachshund's pregnancy lasts 63 days. As the time of birth gets closer, she may show signs of wanting to build her nest. You can help by providing a roomy *whelping box* for the birth. Be sure it's no higher than six inches—remember, your dachshund has short legs! Put some burlap or crumpled newspapers in the bottom to make it comfortable.

Unlike cats, most dogs don't try to hide when they have their pups. But you might see some changes in your female dog's behavior. One dachshund owner noticed that his dog was attracted to soft toys that looked like puppies. Other owners have seen their dogs hide food or become more aggressive than usual. Like humans, each canine mother-to-be behaves in her own way.

When the big day arrives, the birthing can take from one to twelve hours. The puppies arrive either head first or feet first. Both positions are normal. Each newborn comes in a fluid-filled birth sac. The mother first bites

Dachshund puppies grow quickly and begin running around in only a few weeks.

through the sac to free the puppy. Then she bites off its *umbilical cord* and begins licking it clean. This cleaning clears the pup's nose and mouth and stimulates its breathing. Most dachshund litters consist of three to six puppies. The larger the female dog, the larger the litter will probably be.

Sometimes a newborn puppy looks as if it is dead. The mother might handle such a puppy roughly. This is her way of trying to bring it to life. A dog often knows better than her owner whether the puppy will survive. One dachshund breeder thought a puppy was dead and put its body in a stove. Luckily, the fire had gone out. The heat stimulated the pup, and it began to cry.

Puppies are born deaf and blind. Their first instinct is to find their mother's *teats*. They usually manage to do this with only a little help from her. After 10 to 14 days, the pups' eyes open. A week later, they react to sounds, such as their mother's bark. By the time they are about a month old, their 28 milk teeth have come in. Like children's baby teeth, these teeth will be replaced by adult teeth.

During the fourth week, puppies wobble around on their own. They can digest food other than mother's milk. Cow's milk (thinned with water and boiled), soup, rice, and thin mush are good first foods. They can also handle small pieces of tender meat. Before long, meat will be their favorite meal.

As puppies grow, they begin to bark, become more playful, and need their mother less. When they are six weeks old, they can safely be separated from the litter. Now the new dachshund pup is on its way to a new home.

These playful puppies have stopped for a minute to have their picture taken.

SHOWING YOUR DACHSHUND

You're a proud dachshund owner and decide you'd like to enter it in a dog show. There are plenty available, from big, national events to local shows where amateur dog handlers can feel at ease. In *obedience and field trials*, dogs are judged on their abilities and training. In other shows, dogs are judged on how their appearance compares to the best standards for its breed. These are the easiest to enter.

An all-breed show is for dogs from all breeds recognized by the American Kennel Club. First a dog competes within its breed to be "Best of Breed." Then it competes with winners from other breeds to be "Best in Show." Judges use a point system to evaluate each contestant.

A "specialty show" is for dogs of only one breed. The Dachshund Club of America organizes shows just for dachshunds. You don't have to be a member to enter your dog. For boys and girls who are 10 through 16 years old, there is a special classification called "junior handling." Becoming a junior handler can help you learn how to show your dog.

The best way to get used to dog shows is to visit one with your dog. Then try entering a

A dachshund has to look and feel its best to win a ribbon at a show.

match show. These events don't award points. But they help young dogs and new handlers get used to facing competition.

Before your first show, make sure your dog has had its shots. Learn to groom the dog carefully and train it well. It's a good idea to learn the American Kennel Club standards for dachshunds, which judges use to pick winners.

Handling means presenting a dog to be judged. The judges will check its mouth, coat, body build, and other features. You will also

41

have to walk the dog around a ring so its *gait* can be judged.

If you think you'd like to show your dachshund, start training it early. Begin by grooming the dog on a table so it can get used to the process. Help the dachshund to learn to stand straight and still. It might resist, but be patient. Judges will also check a dog's mouth. To help your dachshund get used to this, open its mouth often and have friends do it, too.

On the day of the show, dress casually and arrive early. You'll need to exercise your dog and add last-minute grooming touches.

During the show, listen carefully to the judge so that you can help your dog go through its paces smartly. Your dachshund's success depends on its qualities as a dachshund—and on yours as a loving owner and competent handler.

A DAY AT THE RACES

Ten dachshunds—miniatures, standards, wire-haireds, long-haireds, and "smooths"— bark excitedly behind the starting line. All of them wear brightly colored felt racing coats.

It's the "free-for-all," the last race of the day. Earlier the dogs competed in races two at a time. Now the winners will compete for the grand prize. The owners and spectators are almost as excited as the dachshunds. Favored to win is Gretchen, a wire-haired female in a lemon-yellow coat.

The idea of dachshund racing began at an all-breed dog show in Connecticut in 1966. People were used to seeing sleek *whippets* and *greyhounds* race—but dachshunds? It was hard to imagine these funny, short-legged sausage dogs as racers! But, everyone agreed, it would be good for a laugh.

The dachshunds surprised nearly everyone. They turned out to be natural racers. Their speed and spirit impressed even the whippet owners, who had to train their dogs to race.

Now they're off! Gretchen takes an early lead. But Little Leroy, a miniature smooth-hair, is hot on her heels. As he runs, his ears flop like wings. Right behind him is Pummel, a sturdy black-and-tan. They dash down the 180-yard course, which is outlined by colorful flags. They're chasing after a *lure*, which for this race is a piece of rabbit fur. The lure moves just in front of them on a pulleylike device.

In the home stretch, a newcomer, Archibald IV, breaks from the back and threatens to take the lead. His stubby legs pound the course as he moves up. He passes Pummel, then edges by Little Leroy. For a moment, he and Gretchen are nose and nose. Then suddenly, in the last five yards, Gretchen surges ahead. To the cheers of the crowd, she stretches across the finish line and lunges toward the lure.

Gretchen is a good-natured family pet most of the time. But when she's racing, the instincts that made her ancestors such determined hunters spur her on.

This beautiful long-haired dachshund has just won a prize.

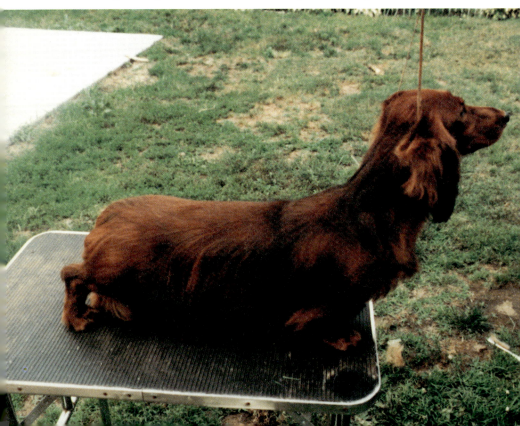

GLOSSARY/ INDEX

Badger 7, 8, 9, 12, 21—A sturdy, burrowing animal with a broad back, short legs, and long claws on its front feet.

Bitch 33—An adult female dog.

Boar 7—A wild hog with a hairy coat and a long snout.

Breed 9, 10, 17, 21, 33, 35, 40—A particular type of dog with common ancestors and similar characteristics. The dachshund is one breed of dog.

Breeder 15, 24, 34, 38—A person who raises and sells animals.

Brindled 13—A coat that has black hairs mixed with white hairs, often in even stripes.

Dappled 13—A coat that has patches of dark color on a lighter background.

Field Trial 40—A contest to show how well a dog can hunt.

Gait 42—The movements of a dog's feet when it is walking, trotting, or running.

Greyhound 43—A tall, slender, smooth-coated dog known for its speed in racing.

Grooming 23, 30, 31—Brushing a dog to keep its coat clean and smooth.

Handling 41—Presenting a dog to be judged in a dog show.

Haw 17—An extra eyelid that helps protect a dog's eye.

Heat 25, 33, 34—The days when a bitch is ready to mate.

Hound Glove 30—A glove with short bristles, wires, or bumps, used to groom dogs.

Housebreaking 29—Training a dog to relieve itself on newspaper or outside the house.

Instincts 20, 44—Natural behaviors that are inborn in a dog.

Litter 24, 25, 38, 39—A family of puppies born at a single whelping.

Lure 43—Bait used to attract animals; also a device, such as an artificial rabbit, that dogs chase during a race.

Muzzle 13—The jaws, nose, and mouth of a dog.

Neuter 34—To operate on a male dog so he can't make a female dog pregnant.

Obedience Trial 40—A contest to show how well a dog has been trained.

Pedigree 24—A chart that lists a dog's ancestors.

Purebred 23, 33—A dog whose ancestors were all of the same breed.

Spay 33—To remove a female dog's ovaries so she can't become pregnant.

Stud 34—A purebred male used for breeding.

Teats 38—A female dog's nipples. Puppies suck on the teats to get milk.

Umbilical Cord 38—A hollow tube that carries nutrients to a puppy while it is inside its mother's body.

Veterinarian 30, 34, 35—A doctor trained to take care of animals.

Whelping Box 36—A roomy box in which a female dog can give birth to her puppies.

Whippet 43—A small, fast, slender dog.

Withers 10—A dog's shoulders; the point where its neck joins the body. A dog's height is measured at the withers.